Razia's Ray of Hope

One Girl's Dream of an Education

Written by
Elizabeth Suneby

Illustrated by
Suana Verelst

WAYLAND
www.waylandbooks.co.uk

One day, my cousins and I noticed men and women were gathering around the empty lot in our village. We raced down the road to see what the excitement was about.

For the courageous women — especially Razia Jan and Patti Quigley —
who work to heal the world, as well as for the brave and enthusiastic
teachers and girls at the Zabuli Education Center in Afghanistan. — E.S.

I dedicate this book to all the courageous girls, women, boys and men
who stand up to adversity and who can make a real and positive change
in the world while remaining true to themselves. — S.V.

First published in this paperback edition by
Wayland © 2016

Text © 2016 Elizabeth Suneby
Illustrations © 2016 Suana Verelst

Acknowledgments
Published by permission of Kids Can Press Ltd.,
Toronto, Ontario, Canada

Heartfelt thanks to the team who
helped me bring Razia's story to life —
Lisa Lyons, Karen Li, Stacey Roderick,
Suana Verelst and Julia Naimska — I
value each of your talents and your
collaborative spirit.
— Elizabeth Suneby

I would like to thank Lisa Lyons and
Karen Li for giving me the opportunity to illustrate
this most interesting and important project. A
heartfelt thank you to Julia Naimska and Stacey
Roderick for all the help and advice along the
way. A special thank you to Liz Suneby, whose
story inspired me to illustrate this beautiful and
mysterious country and its people. And finally a very
special thank you to Razia Jan for her courageous
and important work in Afghanistan. — Suana Verelst

Designed by Julia Naimska

Page 30: Photo courtesy of
Karen Wong Photography
(www.karenwong-photo.com)

ISBN 978 0 7502 9578 9

Printed in China

10 9 8 7 6 5 4 3 2 1

Ribbons brightened the dry earth, men were laying a large stone on the ground, and women were handing out chocolates.

My little sister, Zara, and I collected as many sweets as we could, stuffing them into our pockets before asking for more.

My grandfather, Baba gi, announced:
"This is where my school once stood. It was destroyed by seventeen years of war."
"What is happening today?" I asked.
"Razia, they are building a new school... for girls," said Baba gi.
"I must go!" I cried. Every night I fell asleep dreaming about going to school like my brothers. "Please, Baba gi, ask Baba and Aziz if I may go to school."

That evening, I sat with my youngest brothers while they studied.

"Jamil, may I have a piece of paper?" I asked.

"Why do you need paper? You can't even write," said Karim.

I *could* write! I had memorised my letters and I could write my name. But I was afraid to tell my brothers. What if they would not let me sit with them? I kept quiet.

Whenever I found Baba gi alone, I would whisper in his ear, "Have you spoken to Baba and Aziz yet?"

"I will. I will, my dear Razia," he would say.

So I turned to my mother for help. "Bibi, did you know they are building a school for girls on the empty lot?"
"Yes, I know," Bibi answered, as we walked to the village tandoor to bake naan for dinner.
"Please, Bibi, I want to go to school. Please talk to Baba and Aziz!"

"I will. I will," she said.

Months passed but neither Bibi nor Baba gi ever had an answer. At the beginning of March, the school was nearly ready. Its white walls shone in the sunlight and its red door glowed as brightly as the flames of the tandoor.

Each afternoon, as I fetched water from the well, I saw girls on their way home from registration. They each carried crisp, new uniforms over their arms. I longed to be one of them.

One night, as I lay on my mattress, I heard Baba gi call my father, brothers and uncles to a family meeting. I listened eagerly.

Baba gi started the jerga.

"Razia wants to go to school and I support her desire."

"Before war tore our country apart, women in Afghanistan were educated. They were doctors, government workers and journalists. It is time to give our daughters and granddaughters the chance to read and write. Our family and our country will be stronger for it."

I could not believe my ears. Would I be allowed to go to school?

"Our girls need to help their mothers at home," said my Uncle Iqbal.

"We need Razia to work in the orchards too," Uncle Ali added.

"She can complete her chores before and after school," Baba gi replied.

"Next, you'll want Razia to go into town to shop by herself," said my father.

"Or for women to remove their burqas in public," my brother, Ahmad, added.

My brother Aziz ended the jerga.
"Razia is not going."
Those four simple words made my heart sink.

The next morning, after my morning chores, I walked to the school and knocked on the bright, red door. A woman opened it and greeted me with a smile.

"Hello, my name is Razia Jan. Come in, please."

Inside, there were fresh white hallways, clean classrooms with desks, chalkboards, books, paper and pencils.

"Hello, my name is Razia, too. I want to come to your school, but my brother and father will not let me."

Razia Jan offered to come home with me and speak to Baba gi. Maybe together they could convince Baba and Aziz to let me go to school.

As soon as we arrived home, I ran off to find Baba gi.

"Baba gi, the maulim shabia from the new girls' school is here to speak to you! Please come and greet her."

Baba gi and Razia Jan spoke privately for several minutes. Then, Baba gi went to find my father and mother.

Razia Jan described to Baba and Bibi how her school would teach Dari, English, Pashto, maths, health and hygiene to younger girls. As the girls got older, they would learn how to read the Koran, as well as geography, science and history.

The school would provide textbooks, a new uniform and healthy lunches for all students, too. Best of all, she said, the school would be free.

Just then, my brother, Aziz, walked in.
Razia Jan introduced herself to him. She knew
Aziz was the one she needed to convince.
   "I ask you for your tolerance, if not support,
for Razia's education. Please consider, if men are
the backbone of Afghanistan, then women are
the eyes of our country. Without an education,
we will all be blind."

Aziz shook Razia Jan's hand
and walked out of the room.
I followed him.

"Agha jan, are you feeling sick?" I asked.
His face was pale and sweaty.
"Yes, I have a fever. I have some medicine,
but I need Karim or Jamil to read the instructions
to me," he said.
I poured Aziz a glass of water and, while he
rested, I slowly sounded out the instructions
on the medicine bottle.

"How do you know how to read?" Aziz asked.

"I listen to Jamil and Karim study every night," I said, counting out his pills. "Please, Agha jan, please let me go to school. I will be able to help the family even more if I do."

Aziz took his medicine and smiled. Then he went back to rest without uttering a word.

One day, as I sat on the step peeling potatoes, I heard Aziz approaching.

"Razia," he said. "This morning, I learned that stones from my quarry are being used to build a wall around the girls' school." Aziz paused. "Now I trust that you will be safe in that building, my precious sister. You may attend Razia Jan's school."

I leapt up and threw my arms around Aziz.

"But you must complete your household chores before and after classes," Aziz continued.

"I will not let you down, Agha jan. Thank you! Thank you!" I cried.

On the first day of school, my teacher asked each of us to say our name and what we wanted to be when we grew up.

My friend Sara spoke first.
"Maulim shabia, my name is Sara and I want to be an engineer when I grow up."
Rahila waved her arms and our teacher picked her next.
"I am Rahila, and I want to be a doctor. I will build a clinic in our village and treat all the children for free."

I spoke last.
"Maulim shabia, I have always dreamed of being a teacher. And I promised my mother and my oldest brother, Aziz, that I would practise on them."

Education for Everyone

You might sometimes wish you didn't have to go to school. But can you imagine if you weren't ever *allowed* to go to school? If you never learned how to read or write?

Around the world, about 69 million school-age children are not in school. That's more than the number of people living in the United Kingdom — and more than double the population of Canada!

Almost half of these children (31 million) live in sub-Saharan Africa. More than a quarter (18 million), like Razia, live in Southern Asia. There are many reasons why these children do not go to school, including poverty, political instability, regional conflict and natural disaster. Many children are also kept out of school because their local traditions forbid it. Instead of learning in school, children often must help to support their families, usually by working in jobs that earn very little money.

Razia's story is inspired by the lives of real girls living in the village of Deh'Subz, north of Afghanistan's capital city, Kabul. Only about a quarter of girls living in developing countries go to school at all. And in Afghanistan, only about 13 per cent of women are literate, which means only 13 out of 100 can read and write.

Imagine if your mother couldn't read or write. She wouldn't be able to read you a story, a map or the directions on a medicine bottle. She wouldn't be able to drive a car because she couldn't pass the written test. And there are few well-paying jobs for people who can't read or write, so it's likely your family would not have very much money. By contrast, women who are literate tend to have better incomes, housing and health care. And in turn, they provide these things for their families and communities. Everyone benefits from educating women.

The Real Razia Jan

Razia Jan was born in Afghanistan and moved to the United States of America when she was a young woman. She worked hard as a tailor and raised her son in a small town in Massachusetts.

After the terrorist attacks on 11 September 2001, Razia felt she needed to connect people from her homeland in Afghanistan and people from her new home in America. In 2007, she started Razia's Ray of Hope Foundation. She hoped to improve the lives of women and children in Afghanistan through education.

In 2008, Razia made the big decision to give up her comfortable life in the United States and move back to Kabul, Afghanistan. She planned to open the Zabuli Education Center for Girls. The education center is in the middle of seven villages that never had a girls' school before.

Today, the center is full of 500 young girls learning to read and write. "The students love school so much," says Razia, "that they run in the door every day and even beg for school to be all year long, without vacation. Many of the girls take their workbooks home and teach their mothers the lessons! These brave young girls and their commitment to become educated are the inspiration for this book."

In recognition of Razia's work, she was honored by CNN as one of their Top 10 Heroes of 2012, an award given to ordinary people doing extraordinary things to make the world a better place.

Razia believes that education is the key to positive, peaceful change in the world. Do you agree?

Razia Jan with students Parwana, Bibi Ayesha and Bibi Begum. These best of friends are among the top students in their class.

Dari Words

Agha jan: a title of respect

Baba: Father

Baba gi: Grandfather

Bibi: Mother

burqa: the wrap some Muslim women must wear in public to cover themselves fully from head to toe, even their faces

Dari: one of the official languages spoken in Afghanistan, along with Pashto

jerga: a decision-making meeting held by the eldest men in the family

maulim shabia: literally, "Miss Teacher"

naan: the traditional flat bread eaten in Afghanistan and many other countries in South and Central Asia

Pashto: one of the official languages spoken in Afghanistan, along with Dari

registration: to sign up to go to school

salam alekum: the words for both "hello" and "peace"

tandoor: a clay oven used for cooking and baking foods, including naan

Classroom Activities: A Day in Razia's Life

The activities below are designed to help students:
- compare the lives of girls where they live to the lives of girls in Afghanistan
- understand the importance of education and, in particular, educating girls
- consider how they can help children around the world receive an education.

Girls in School

Activity: Have the girls in your class stand up. Ask 60 per cent (3 out of 5) of the girls to sit down. Explain that they are not lucky enough to attend primary school in Afghanistan. Of the remaining 40 per cent still standing, ask 80 per cent (4 out of 5) of those girls to sit. Explain that these girls are not able to finish their schooling. The girls left standing are approximately the number of girls who are actually able to complete a primary-school education in Afghanistan.

QUESTIONS FOR DISCUSSION:
- How many girls in your class expect to finish (infant, junior, secondary) school?
- How does it make you feel that many girls in Afghanistan and other countries are not able to attend school?
- How do you think these girls' lives will be different from the lives of girls who attend your school?

A Typical School Day

Ask students to write down their typical school day. Once they have finished, ask a couple of students to share with the class how their lives are different from those of the girls in Razia's school.

Compare and Contrast:
- chores before and after school
- travel to and from school — length of time and mode of transportation
- who prepares dinner
- electricity supply, and how that affects studying and bedtime

Necessities versus Extras

Activity: Ask students to write down a list of items and activities they spend money on. These should be things that are nice to have, but not necessary (for example, designer clothing, posters, concert tickets, phones, music downloads, fast food, movies and sweets, popcorn and drinks). Then have them add up the annual amount they spend on these extras. After they have done so, share with them the approximate donation needed to educate a girl for one year at Razia's school in Afghanistan.

Annual expenses for a student at Razia's school	Cost (£)
Tuition (pays for building maintenance, teachers' salaries, books, etc.)	133
Uniform (two uniforms, shoes and headscarf)	33
Pencils	0.67
Notebooks	1.33
Total	168

QUESTIONS FOR DISCUSSION:
- In one year, how does the cost of your 'extras' compare to the cost of Razia's education?
- What items and activities can you think of that are 'nice to have' that cost about the same as a year of school in a developing country?
- How can you use this information to help young people around the world receive an education? Some food for thought: You and your friends might save or raise money to donate by volunteering your time, skills and talents (for example, raking leaves and organising bake sales). Or perhaps you could spread the word on the issue of illiteracy and the importance of education (for example, writing articles in the school paper).

These activities have been adapted and used with permission from the Razia's Ray of Hope Foundation, **www.raziasrayofhope.org**.